MISHMA

COOL AS A CUCUMBER

little bee books

little bee books

An imprint of Bonnier Publishing USA
853 Broadway, New York, New York 10003
Copyright © 2017 by Bonnier Publishing USA
Manufactured in China   RRD 1116
First Edition
2 4 6 8 10 9 7 5 3 1
ISBN 978-1-4998-0374-7

littlebeebooks.com
bonnierpublishingusa.com

ARE YOU READY FOR A

MISH-MASH

OF COOL ACTIVITIES?

HERE WE GO!

Can you get the soup to Suzy's stomach?

Sherry is celebrating and needs an appropriate dessert.

Use this guide to color in the squares and find out what it is.

3 = ☐ 9 = ☐

4 = ■ 12 = ■

7 = ■ 14 = ☐

FOOD CODE:

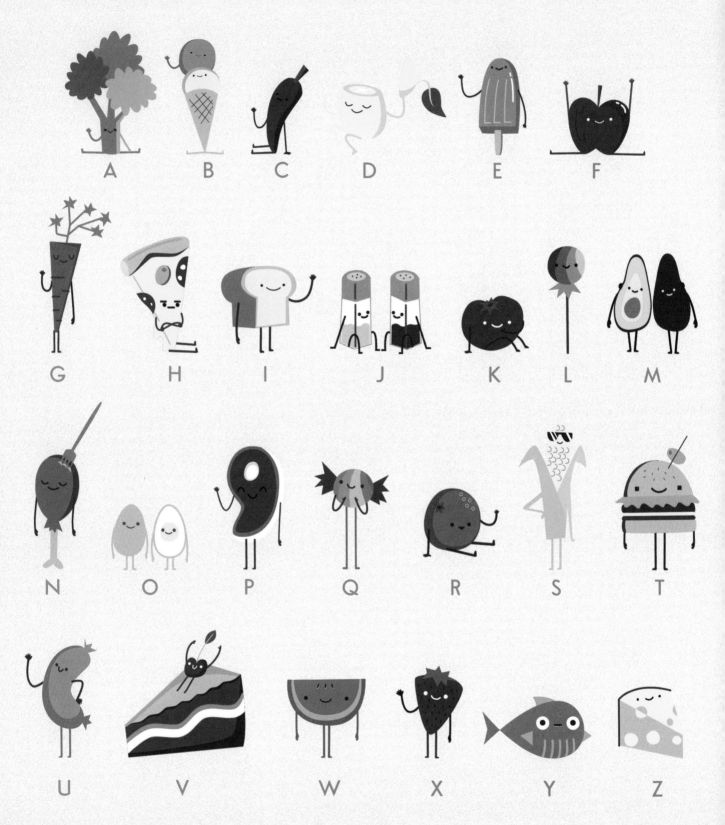

A B C D E F

G H I J K L M

N O P Q R S T

U V W X Y Z

This chef has dough, cheese, sauce, and pepperoni. What do you think he's making?

_____

What did the snake eat?

Follow the path to find out.

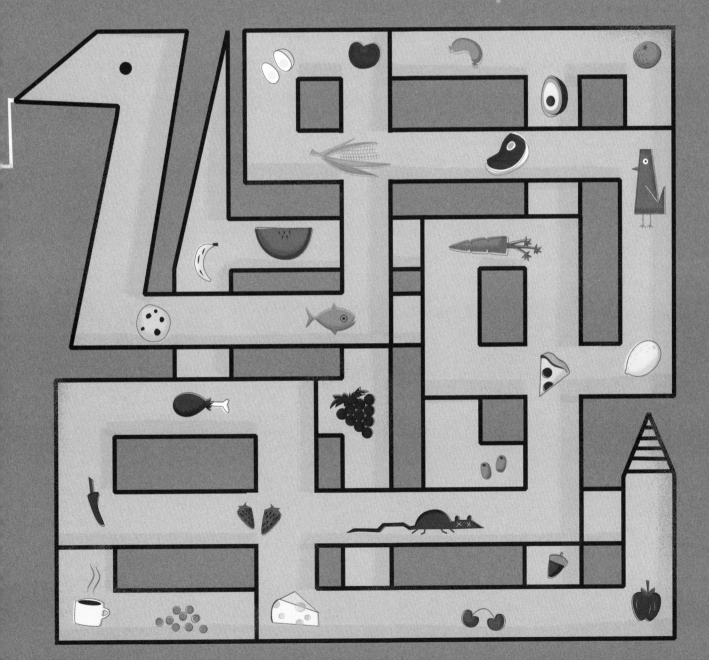

Grid Drawing

	A	B	C	D	E
1					
2					
3					
4					
5					
6					

D6	C1	A4	D5	A1
A6	D4	B6	E6	B5
A5	C3	B4	E5	E1
B1	E3	C6	D2	D1
C5	C2	D3	B3	A3
E4	A2	E2	C4	B2

$2.00 $1.00 $1.50 $2.00

$1.50 $5.00 $4.50 $2.50

Welcome to the
Monster Supermarket!

Look at the prices above and
figure out how much the groceries
on the conveyor belts will cost.

Your Pizza Is Ready!
Help the deliveryman get the
hot pizza to the house.

Now color the pizza party!

DRAW A PICTURE OF THE PIZZA PARTIERS AFTER THEY'RE ALL FULL OF PIZZA.

HOW TO DRAW A SQUID

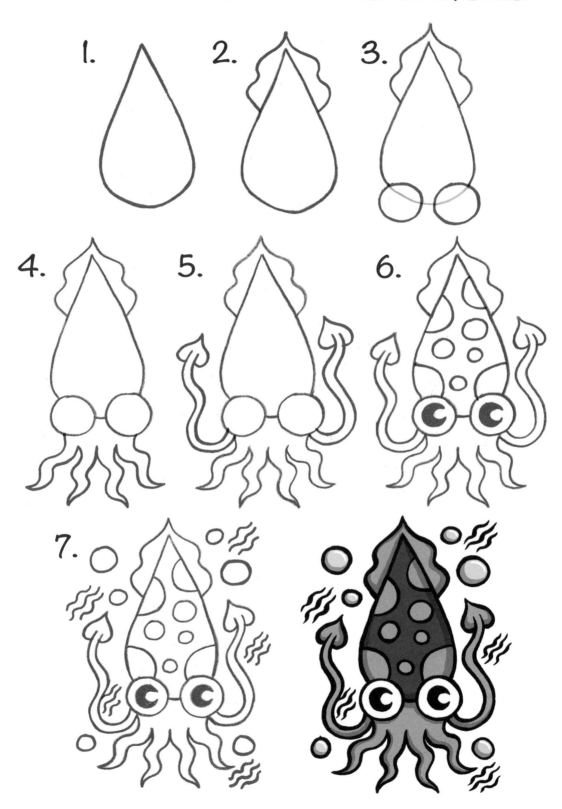

1.
2.
3.
4.
5.
6.
7.

Turn the page to find out!

Q: WHY DID THE COOKIE GO TO THE DOCTOR?

A: BECAUSE IT WAS FEELING CRUMMY.

These guys are both looking pale.
Give them some color!

Help Hansel get through the forest to Gretel, following a path up, down, left, or right, moving between icons that are either the same shape or color.

Add some toppings to this ice cream sundae.

Crayons

Cell Phone

Onion

Celery

Boot

Baseball

Rocks

Chicken

Flashlight

Carrots

Basketball

What do you think the chef should put in his soup?

Balloons

Bike Wheel

Clams

Salt & Pepper

Stapler

List these foods in alphabetical order:

_____

_____

_____

_____

_____

_____

_____

_____

Eggs

Green Beans

Lemon

Ice Cream

Herbs

Donut

Apple

Corn

Nachos

Kale

Orange

Falafel

Banana

Macaroni

Lettuce

Give the rest of these party animals festive hats!

SUGAR

WATER

BAKING POWDER

Study this page, and then turn to page 36.

MILK

EGGS

BUTTER

FLOUR

CHOCOLATE

COLOR THE FRUIT ON THIS LITTLE GUY'S BIG SHIRT.

Turn the page to find out!

Q: WHAT DO YOU GIVE A SICK LEMON?

A: LEMON AID

GERMANY

JAPAN

ITALY

ENGLAND

FRANCE

CHINA

FOODS OF THE WORLD | Pick out the image that doesn't fit in.

Do you know where our food comes from? Some fruits and vegetables are grown by farmers.

Let's find out how they're grown.

First the farmer needs to make sure that the soil is ready to grow the fruits or vegetables. This is done by "tilling"—which is turning the soil over so fresh soil is on top.

Some farmers use tractors to do this.

Once the farmer has tilled the soil, it's time to start planting the seeds.

This is also called "sowing" seeds.

It's important to do this at the right time of year. Some fruits and vegetables grow best in the summer and others in the winter.

SEED

It's really important to keep the seeds watered, so the fruits and vegetables can grow.

It can take a long time for the seeds to start growing. You need to have a lot of patience.

After several months, it's time to pick the crops. This is called "harvesting."

Do you remember all the items from page 30?

List them here:

_____

_____

_____

_____

_____

_____

_____

_____

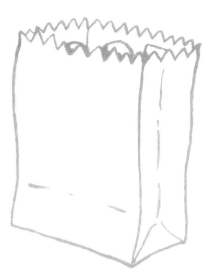

If you have all of these ingredients, you can make a chocolate cake!

Draw one here.

How much do you think
the items below should cost?

Fill in the prices to complete the menu.

M E N U

It's harvest time at the Monster Orchard, but something's not quite right. Some fruits and vegetables grow on trees, and some grow on or under the ground.

Can you pick out which items don't actually grow on trees?

Give this poem a title.

_____

The Sugar Queen Fairy was in a tizzy.
"My lemon-lime soda is no longer fizzy!
Now who would drink a concoction like that?
I need a drink with bubbles—not one that's flat!"

The little fruit fairies all rushed to the throne
when they heard the queen complain and moan.
They tried and tried to add some bubbles,
but all they did was find more troubles.

But then the royal jester walked in,
and on his face was a big, wide grin.
He then grabbed the glass and saved the day
by fixing the problem in a brilliant way.

Turn the page to find out!

Q: WHAT DO YOU CALL 200 STRAWBERRIES BUNCHED TOGETHER?

A: STRAWBERRY JAM

FREAKY FOODS
TRUE OR FALSE

In Thailand, people eat grasshoppers.

In Japan, people eat crackers filled with wasps.

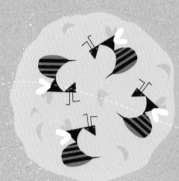

In France, people eat snails.

In Australia, people eat kangaroos.

In the United States, people eat rattlesnakes.

A: All of them are true!

GRID DRAWING

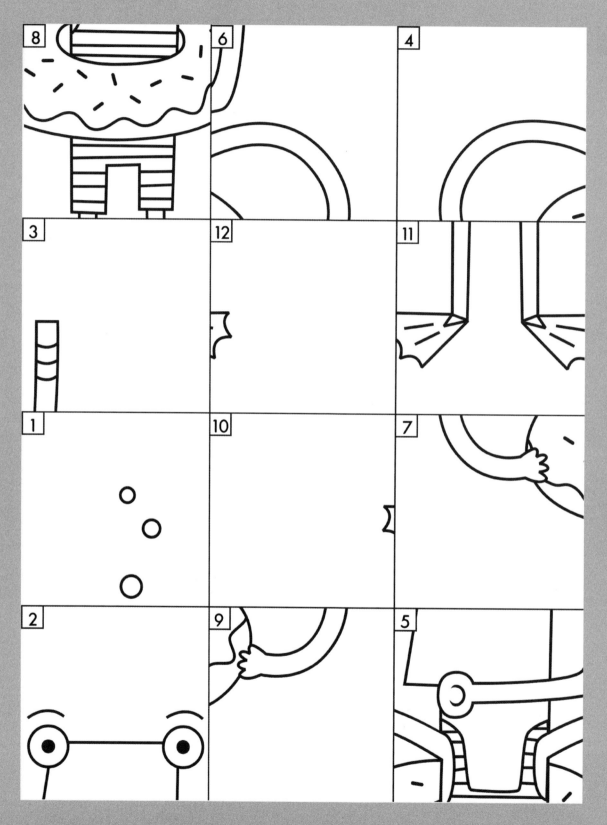

Draw in the matching shape from the grid on the left to reveal the scrambled image.

1	2	3
4	5	6
7	8	9
10	11	12

PIZZA TIME!

Add toppings to the pizza.

Connect the dots.

Fill this blender with everything you need to make your dream food.

Now draw the final product!

What do you think Billy ate?

Draw it below.

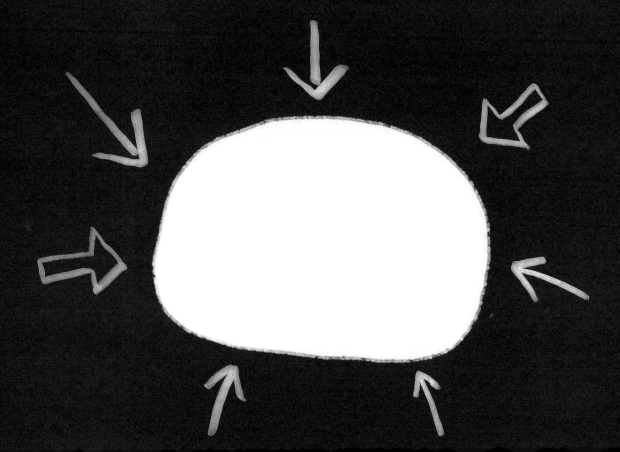

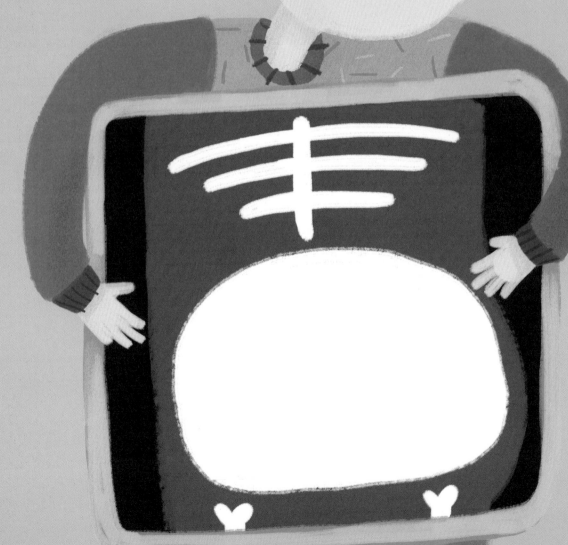

Hold this page up to the light to reveal Billy's x-ray.

You were right Why would he eat that?

52

* DRAW A PICTURE OF BANANA ON THE BLANK PAPER.

HOW TO DRAW A MERMAID

1.
2.
3.
4.
5.
6.
7.

Q: WHAT'S AN ELEPHANT'S FAVORITE VEGETABLE?

Turn the page to find out!

A: SQUASH

This caterer is lost and needs help getting the cake to the party!

What's in the magician's hat?

What's in this man's soup?

Connect the dots to find out!

Give this party some color!

PICNIC PREDICAMENT

Carrie is confused! She has unpacked her basket, but some items are missing!
Can you help her look for them?

HOW TO DRAW A RACE CAR

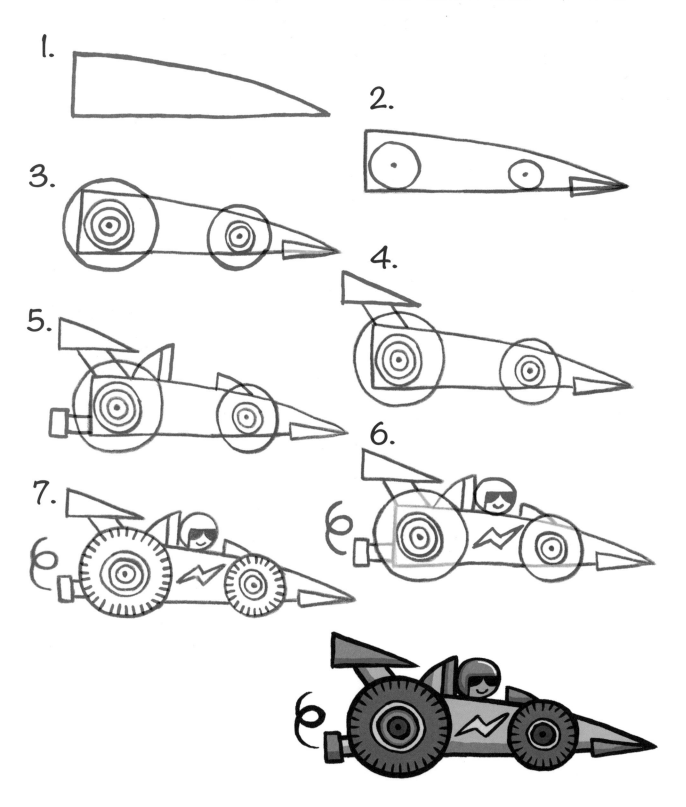

1.

2.

3.

4.

5.

6.

7.

Turn the page to find out!

Q: WHY DID THE STUDENTS EAT THEIR HOMEWORK?

A: BECAUSE THE TEACHER SAID
THAT IT WAS A PIECE OF CAKE.

Quick! Color these guys before they come tumbling down!

Give these men some mustaches.

FANTASTIC FLIP BOOKS

FOLLOW THESE DIRECTIONS TO ASSEMBLE YOUR OWN FLIP BOOK!

STEP 1: CAREFULLY CUT OUT EACH FLIP BOOK PAGE ALONG THE BLACK LINES.

STEP 2: PUT THE PAGES IN ORDER. TAP THE PICTURE EDGE ON A FLAT SURFACE.

BINDER CLIP ←

STEP 3: USING A BINDER CLIP, BIND THE OPPOSITE EDGE OF THE FLIP BOOK.

STEP 4: FLIP THROUGH THE PAGES TO BRING THE CHARACTERS TO LIFE!

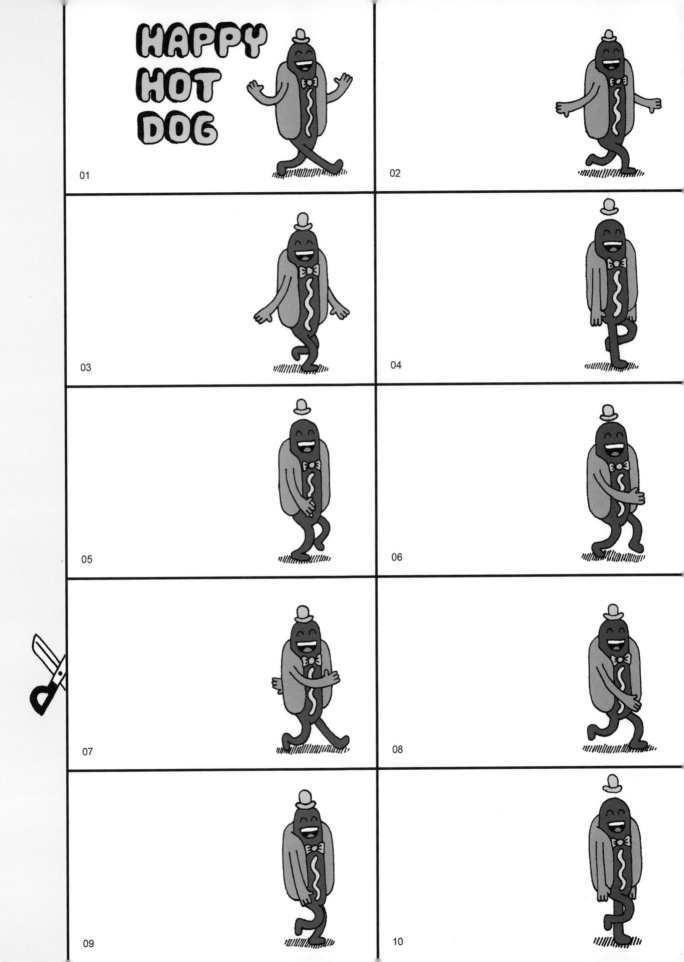

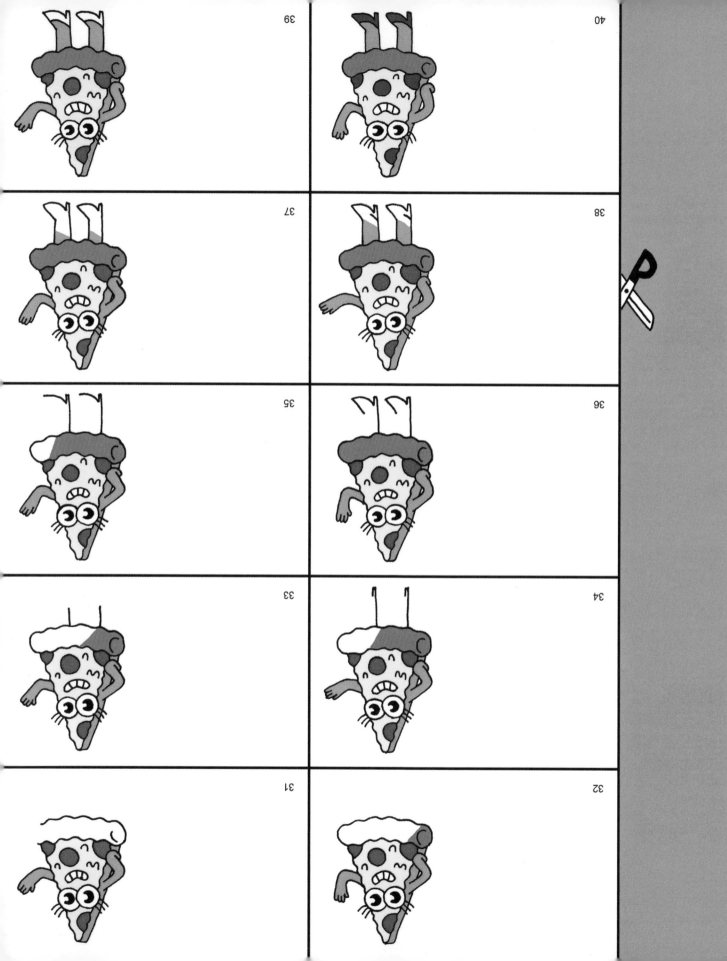

11

12

13

14

15

16

17

18

19

20

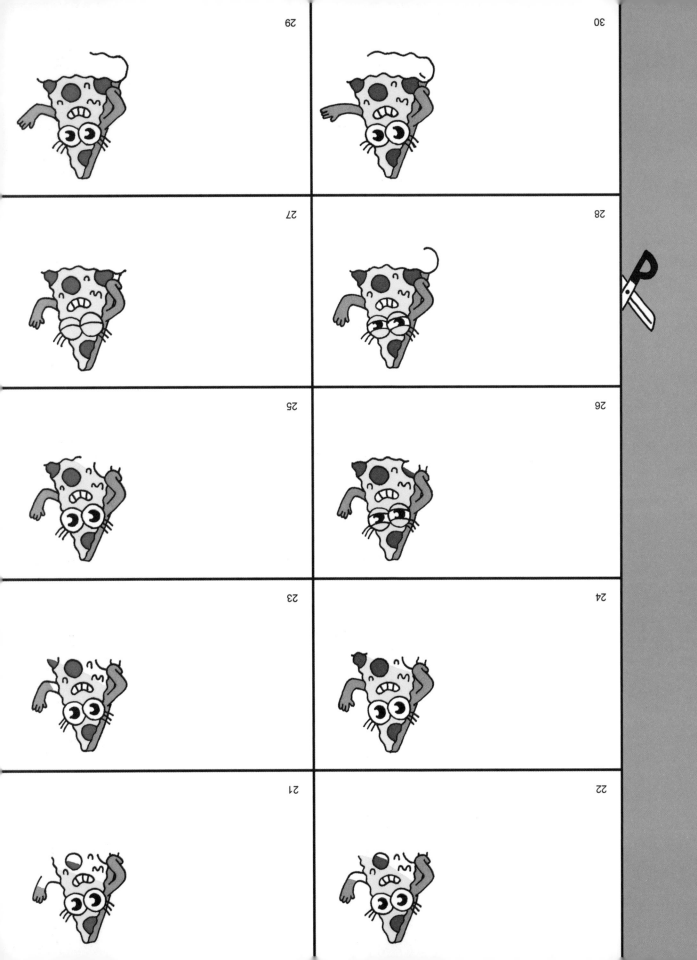

21

22

23

24

25

26

27

28

29

30

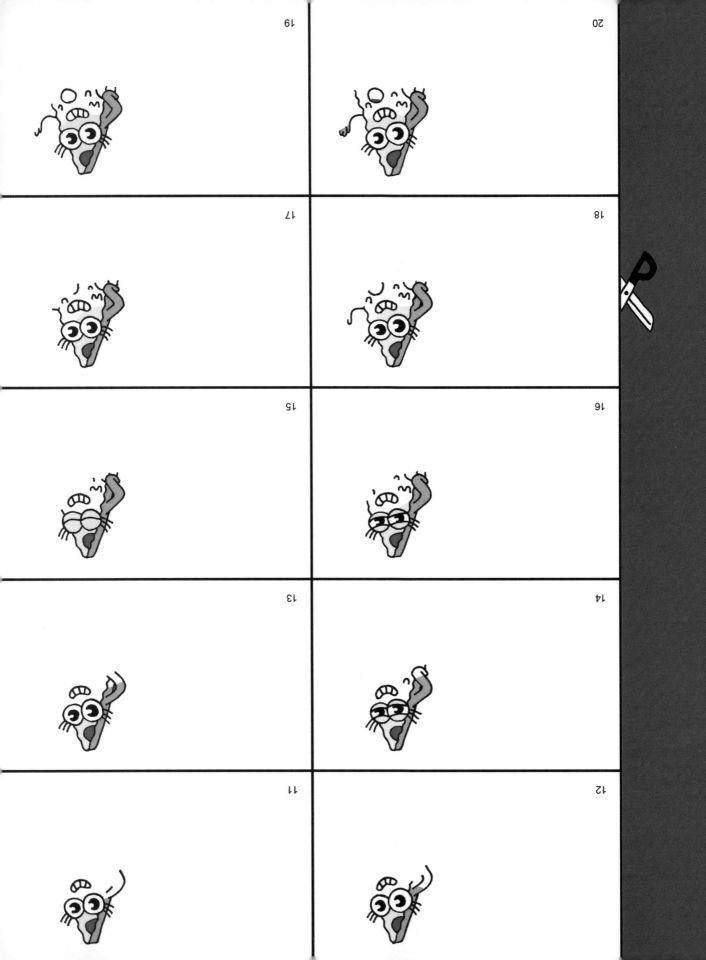

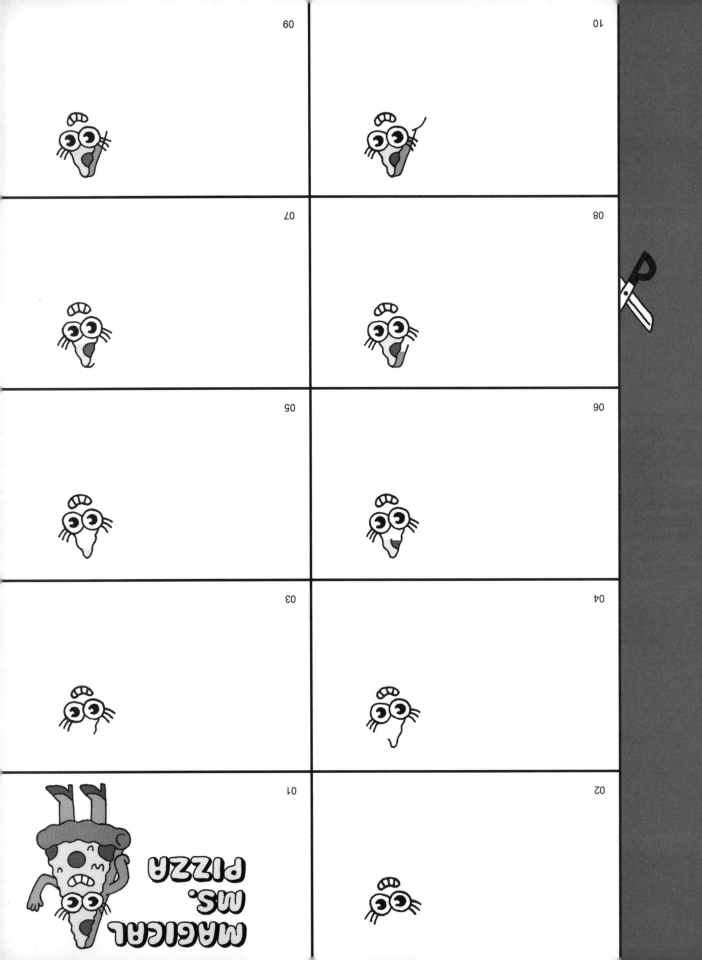

COOKING CONUNDRUM

Find the path that connects these tasty foods to their chefs.

Turn the page to find out!

Q: WHAT DAY DO POTATOES HATE THE MOST?

* DRAW YOUR OWN MYSTERY FLOWER.

Here's the beginning of a story. YOU can write the ending!

Anna and Steve were getting ready
for their mom's birthday party.
Anna strung together some balloons
and tied them to a chair.
"Now we just need to set the table
and get the cake from Mrs. Owen."

"I'll get the cake! I'll get the cake!" said Steve.
"Uh . . ." started Anna.
"I can do it!" cried Steve. "She's
just a few doors down, and
I promise I'll be careful."
"Well . . . okay. But whatever you do,
don't drop it!" warned Anna.

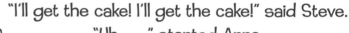

Steve ran out the door and was at Mrs. Owen's in no time.
She handed him the cake. It smelled so yummy!

"Be careful now, Stevie," she said with a smile.
"I will!" promised Steve.

Steve started to walk back slowly,
when he spotted his friend Bruce on his skateboard.
Bruce was coming right at him!

"Hey Steve! Look *ouuut!*"

Steve jumped out of the way, but the cake went flying out of his arms and landed...

_____

_____

_____

_____

_____

_____

Now illustrate your ending below.

Color these little guys

and their funny hats!

Can you spot the nine things missing on the right page?

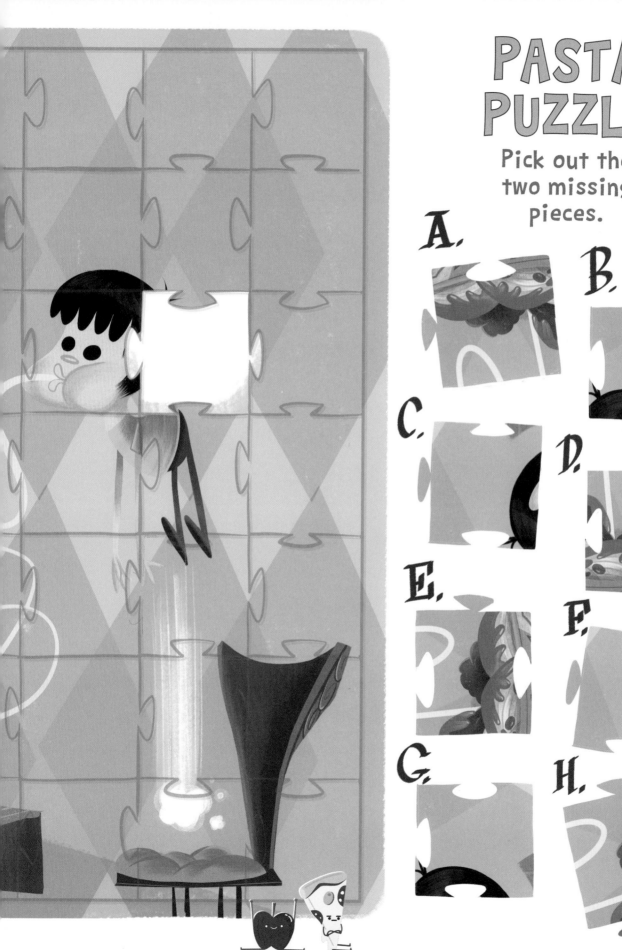

PASTA PUZZLE

Pick out the two missing pieces.

A.

B.

C.

D.

E.

F.

G.

H.

This pig sure is cool! Give him some color.

Now draw him a cool pig girlfriend.

Give this fella a fancy hat.

PERPLEXING PATTERNS

GOOD LUCK FINDING YOUR WAY THROUGH THESE PATTERNS

Start

Finish

START

FINISH

103

Can you spot these foods in the monster's belly?

Turn the page to find out!

Q: WHY WAS THE CUCUMBER MAD?

Draw some heavy things
for this strongman to lift.

CONTRIBUTORS

Celeste Aires is an illustrator from Argentina who is mad about geometry. She does mostly editorial work, advertising, poster art and experimental animation. Her art style has a mix of mid-century and modern that is strongly geometrical, has a minimal color palette, and is full of silly characters.
(pages 1, 6-9, 31, 33, 43-45, 92-93, 112, & cover)

Lisa Perrett enjoys illustrating for kids' media and designing imaginative branding for businesses, inspired daily by her two daughters, with whom she resides along with her husband in the forever young city of Charleston, South Carolina.
(pages 3-5, 18-19, 32, 40, 42, 56, 74, 90)

Alex Chiu is a professional cartoonist who currently lives in Portland, Oregon. He has worked with galleries, publishers, and clothing companies, creating works of art using his signature cartooning style. Alex also teaches classes and workshops in drawing, cartooning, and animation throughout the Portland area. (pages 16, 53-54, 72, 78-86, 89)

Paco Sordo is a Spanish freelance illustrator with more than a decade of experience working in comics, animation, advertising, and picture books. His clients include Nickelodeon, Rovio, Cartoon Network, and Hallmark among others. His heart is divided between his two passions: drawing and pizza.
(pages 58-63, 67, 87, 94-97)

Jean Claude is a self-taught illustrator from Manchester, UK. While he's most at home with his drawing tablet and a cup of strong coffee, Jean also enjoys long walks with his dog, Ted, preparing elaborate meals, and visiting the zoo for artistic inspiration! (pages 14, 50-52, 56, 75, 88, 98, 106)

Barroux studied photography, art, sculpture, and architecture in France at the famous École Estienne and École Boulle. He began illustrating by creating linocut images, and continues to try out various techniques in his work—from collages with antique paper, to oil pastels. When creating art, he always tries to surprise the little kid that is inside of him.
(pages 20-21, 28-29, 64-65, 76-77, 100-101, 108-109)

Erica Salcedo studied fine arts at the University of Castilla-La Mancha before obtaining a master's degree in graphic design and illustration at the Polytechnic University of Valencia. Since graduating, she's worked as an illustrator on projects with publishers around the world. (pages 26-27, 47-49, 68-71, 104-105, 107)

Dan Fenelon is an artist, muralist, illustrator, and graphic designer. His many public artworks can be seen at museums, libraries, schools, community centers, performing art centers, and hospitals. Dan is also the operator and resident artist of the Montclair Art Museum Art Truck, with which he travels New Jersey facilitating amazing interactive public art projects with anyone who is willing to participate. (pages 22-25)

Adam Pryce is a freelance illustrator based in Manchester, UK. His artwork is fun and colorful—confidently working in both digital and hand-drawn techniques. He loves printmaking and regularly leads creative workshops around the UK—working with people of all ages and learning difficulties. Adam loves to draw animals (his favorite animals being cats and bears, and most recently cheeky tigers). His most beloved items are his silver shoes which he wears daily. (pages 10-13, 30, 34-35, 37-39, 46, 66)

THE END

LOOK FOR THESE OTHER MISHMANIA BOOKS

Rain, Rain, Go Away!
ISBN: 978-1-4998-0373-0

Monster Madness
ISBN: 978-1-4998-0375-4

Hit the Road!
ISBN: 978-1-4998-0376-1